Miss Dirt the Dustman's Daughter

by ALLAN AHLBERG

with pictures by
TONY ROSS

PUFFIN

PUFFIN BOOKS

Published by the Penguin Group
Penguin Books Ltd, 80 Strand, London WC2R 0RL, England
Penguin Group (USA), Inc., 375 Hudson Street, New York, New York 10014, USA
Penguin Books Australia Ltd, 707 Collins Street, Melbourne, Victoria 3008, Australia
Penguin Books Canada Ltd, 10 Alcorn Avenue, Toronto, Ontario, Canada M4V 3B2
Penguin Books India (P) Ltd, 11 Community Centre, Panchsheel Park, New Delhi – 110 017, India
Penguin Group (NZ), cnr Airborne and Rosedale Roads, Albany, Auckland 1310, New Zealand
Penguin Books (South Africa) (Pty) Ltd, Block D, Rosebank Office Park, 181 Jan Smuts Avenue,
Parktown North, Gauteng 2193, South Africa

Penguin Books Ltd, Registered Offices: 80 Strand, London WC2R 0RL, England

puffinbooks.com

First published by Viking 1996
Published in Puffin Books 1996
026

Text copyright © Allan Ahlberg, 1996
Illustrations copyright © Tony Ross, 1996

The moral right of the author and illustrator has been asserted

Manufactured in China

British Library Cataloguing in Publication Data
A CIP catalogue record for this book is available from the British Library

ISBN: 978-0-14037-882-5

Daisy Dirt was an unusual girl.
She was the poorest
and the richest girl
in the whole town.

Daisy had lots to wear
and nothing to wear;
a huge room of her own
and a tiny room of her own.

She had a little dog

and a big dog,

a little hamster
and a big h . . .

horse.

A big dinner . . .
and a *very* big dinner!

You see, Daisy lived
half the time with her dad
and half the time with her mum.

Daisy's dad was a dustman.
He was a divorced dustman on the dole.
"What's 'on the dole' mean, Dad?"
said Daisy.
" 'On the dole' means: out of work –
no money – skint!" her dad said.

Daisy's mum was a duchess.
She had got married again – to a duke.
He was a dozy duke in a Daimler.
"What's a 'Daimler', Mum?" said Daisy.

"This is!" said her mum.

Daisy's life was a whirl.
Here is her diary to prove it.

Monday:

breakfast with Dad
school
tea at Betty Biff's
house
home to Mum

Bett

Tuesday:

breakfast with Mum
school
tea at Maisie Maney's
                house

    home to Dad

And so on.
And so on.
And so on.

Yes, Daisy's life was a whirl.
She went back and forth
between her mum and dad
like a parcel –
like a pendulum –
like a ping-pong ball.

"I never know if I'm coming
or going," she said.

Then one day Daisy went
to her mum's and found . . .

nothing to wear,
nothing to eat –
and no horse!

There was a crowd in the street;
a car-boot sale on the lawn;
FOR SALE signs everywhere.

You see, the duke
had had some bad luck.
He was stony broke.

"What's 'stony broke' mean, Mum?"
said Daisy.
" 'Stony broke' means: no money – skint!"
"Oh dear!" said Daisy.
"Yes," said her mum.
"I'm a down-and-out duchess."

But still Daisy's life was a whirl.
Still she went back and forth
between her mum and dad
like a homing pigeon
(with *two* homes) –

like a hamster in a wheel.

Here is her diary again to prove it.

Saturday:

breakfast with Mum
jumble sale with Mum
bike ride with Mum
home to Dad

Sunday:

breakfast with Dad
washing up with Dad
football match with Dad
home to Mum

And so on.
And so on.
And so on.

Then one day Daisy went
to her dad's and found . . .

a crowd in the street;
a TV reporter at the door;
photographers everywhere.

You see, Daisy's dad
had had some *good* luck.
He had won the Lottery.

Then out they went for a drive . . .

. . . in a Daimler.

Daisy Dirt was an unusual girl.
She was the richest
and the poorest girl
in the whole town.

And she still is.

The End